Contents

THE MAGICAL ADVENTURES OF SQUISHVILLE

Welcome To Squishville

TAIRA FOO

Illustrated by
ANN FOO

TAIRA FOO BOOKS

Dedicated to all the believers out there...

Welcome To Squishville

Squishville

Welcome to Squishville. Grandpa Squish and Grandma Squash live here. These funny little squirrels enjoy telling stories to all their little boy and girl grand-squirrels and their friends, these tiny squirrels are called squishes and squashes.

Squishville is a really special place because it is made up of mushroom houses, each one with different-shaped spots just like a giraffe. Many marvellous characters live here and you will get to meet them all as you read all their magical stories.

Here in Squishville you will find upside-down rainbows, flying sunbeams, sparkly stars, wishy squishy soup and lots more magical things to look out for. It is true that almost all of the little squirrels in Squishville are cheerful, but there is one sad little Squish called Bruni who isn't so squeaky and squirky as the rest. We will come back to Bruni in a minute.

Firstly, I am going to introduce you to a cheeky little Squish called Sausage Pot. I think you will like Sausage Pot – he's a bit naughty, loves food and he's got a great big tummy.

There he is…

"I am always hungry"

Hello everyone! My name is Sausage Pot and I live in this wonderful place called Squishville.

Grandpa Squish really does love to tell us little Squishes and Squashes loads and loads of stories about his life.

Every night I go into Grandpa Squish and Grandma Squash's enormous red mushroom house to listen to stories that will teach me to have courage, be really kind to everyone I meet and be grateful for all the fun stuff we have around us in Squishville. There is loads of magic here too, and Grandpa and Grandma always make sure we find it!

My favourite part of the day is when the flying sunbeams come out in the morning and kiss our mushroom houses. As soon as they kiss our roofs they light up our houses and wake us up so we can start eating.

My mushroom house has lots and lots of things to eat like spotted plops, ping pong mops and ooodgie ma flops. As soon as I open my eyes I bounce all the way down the very steep staircase, push a door heavier than my Daddy Pots and climb up the wonky cupboards to find something to fill my very empty tummy. My smile stretches all the way across my round fuzzy face and it stays there till I have to close my eyes because I am too tired to eat anymore.

At story time tonight, I heard that we are going to learn about a little Squish called Bruni who wasn't getting to eat anything at all. Poor old Bruni – I hope the story ends with him eating absolutely everything…

Thank you and see you at story time! Sausage Pot

ONE

The Squibble

My bottom won't fit

*I*t was 6pm and Grandpa Squish and Grandma Squash gathered all the little Squishes and Squashes in their red mushroom house for story time.

As the little squirrels sat down, Sausage Pot began to squibble with another Squish called Windipops. You can probably guess why he's called that – he has a lot of air in him that likes to escape out of his bottom.

"That's my seat, Windipops," said Sausage Pot.

"Yeah, but it looks so squishy and squashy, Sausage Pot, and I want to sit somewhere different today," said Windipops.

"Nope, there ain't no way I'm going to sit anywhere else because it's not fair. My big bottom is not going to fit on such teeny weeny chairs, Windipops, look," Sausage Pot said as he tried to sit on one of the other chairs.

Oh Dear

Grandpa Squish saw the squibble and walked over to the little Squishes.

"Well what is all this squibbling about, Sausage Pot and Windipops?" he asked.

"Smelly old Windipops is in my seat!" said Sausage Pot.

Windipops looked upset.

"Oh well, then he will have to move, won't he, Sausage Pot?" said Grandpa Squish.

"That is exactly what I have been trying to say, Grandpa Squish," said Sausage Pot with a smug smile.

"As soon as you show me where your name is on

that chair, Sausage Pot, you can tell Windipops to move," said Grandpa Squish.

Sausage Pot froze at first and then frantically looked around the chair to see if he could find his name on it.

"Oh well, erm, it don't seem to be there, Grandpa Squish," Sausage Pot said with his head bowed.

"And besides, look, my bottom won't fit on it," Sausage Pot tried to sit on the chair again but Grandpa Squish could see he was pretending his bottom wouldn't fit.

"I don't think your name is there, Sausage Pot," said Windipops.

"And I think your bottom can fit on that chair over there," said Grandpa Squish, pointing at another seat.

"Well maybe if I breathe in, Grandpa Squish. Anyway, while I was looking for my name I found half of a blue floating spot which tasted lovely. Do you want a bit, Windipops?" Sausage Pot was enjoying the taste of the blue floating spot so much that he sat on Windipops' seat to eat it. His bottom fitted perfectly.

"Oh," said Sausage Pot, with a rather uncomfortable smile covered in a blue floating spot.

Grandpa Squish and Windipops looked at Sausage Pot and waited.

"What?" said Sausage Pot as he licked the remains of the blue floating spot from his mouth.

Still they waited…

"I suppose I am going to have to give up my most favourite seat," said Sausage Pot, reluctantly.

. . .

Grandpa Squish let three seconds pass and said, "Kindness can be one of the most powerful things in the whole wide world, Sausage Pot."

"Why does everything have to be about kindness?" Sausage Pot replied, the smile gone from his face. "I think sometimes you just have to be a bit naughty, Grandpa Squish. You know, change it up a bit, live life on the edge,"

But Grandpa didn't respond and Sausage Pot knew the squibble was over.

"Alright you can have the seat, Windipops. Let's hope you don't blow a hole in it – I really love that chair!" said Sausage Pot.

Oops!

Sausage Pot and Windipops looked at Grandpa Squish and then again at each other. They both felt a bit silly to have squibbled. In fact, Windipops felt so silly that his nerves tightened and he let out a tiny trump.

"Swooooh! What's that smell? Someone's definitely let one go," said Sweet Pea, a tiny Squash sitting on a chair nearby.

Squiggling and giggling inside

All the little Squishes and Squashes knew where the smell was coming from. They looked at Windipops and squiggled and giggled with laughter. Grandpa Squish also squiggled and giggled but he did it inside so that the little Squishes and Squashes couldn't see him doing it. They all looked at Windipops squiggling and giggling and joined in with his laughter.

Grandma Squash

As the Squishes and Squashes took their seats, Grandma Squash was busy making supper. It is always mushroom soup. Grandma Squash's special secret mushroom soup grows blue floating spots as she stirs it, filling the enchanted house with even more magic as the small tasty spots travel through the narrow spaces in the tiny kitchen door and up the twitchy noses of the little squirrels. All the little Squishes and Squashes love the purple glow around each spot but especially love their smell. The blue floating spots smell just like chocolate and ice cream and taste just as good.

Look at her flying

Grandma Squash's small furry feet turn inwards which makes her squirrel body sway from side to side as she walks. Her pink dress is spattered with cake and splashes of soup but the best thing about Grandma Squash is, she joins in with all the fun. She is a grown up and a little bit old but the little squirrels love to see her bouncing and boinging all over Squishville, getting herself into all sorts of scrapes. It makes the little squirrels squiggle and giggle so much that their eyes nearly pop out of their round fuzzy heads. Grandma Squash has probably given away at least a million hugs and a hundred squishkisses. When squirrels kiss they kiss with their huge squidgy cheeks – these are called squishkisses.

Once the Squishes and Squashes finish every last bit of their yummy mushroom soup, Grandpa Squish slowly wobbled over to sit down on his red comfy stool with a huge cup of hot Squashlate in his hands. He began to tell Bruni's story.

Finally I can tell my story

TWO

Storytime

"*O*ne morning in Squishville, as I was taking one of my magnificent walks, I decided that I would try something new and take a different route to my usual walk. It's always good to explore new things, as long as it's safe, mind. While on my walk I noticed a mushroom house that stood away from all the other mushroom houses. It seemed so sad…"

"Why was it sad? Was it hungry?" said Sausage Pot.

"Well, Sausage Pot, I knew it was sad because it was grey, like a big fat cloud that's eaten too much rain and is about to burst!" said Grandpa Squish.

"OOOOOOH yeah," said Sausage Pot. "I know how that feels."

"As I approached the sad little mushroom, my ears felt so heavy they fell on to my shoulders and made me start to droop like a jelly that's being held upside down.

"OOOOOOH jelly! What flavour was it, Grandpa Squish?" said Sausage Pot.

Jelly is my favourite

The little Squishes and Squashes looked at Sausage Pot rubbing his oversized tummy and squiggled and giggled with laughter.

"Then what happened?" said Sausage Pot, ignoring their laughter.

I can smell cabbage and cheese

"Well, Sausage Pot, I made a decision that I would poke my sizeable head into the broken window of this unhappy little mushroom house. First my nose poked in. I could smell cabbage and cheese and it wasn't a very nice smell. It was quite difficult for me to get the next part of my face in due to the size of my cheeks, but because they are so squidgy they managed to squeeze through. It made my eyes water and my tiny spectacles almost fell off my face!

"Eventually I managed to peer through the tiny space and I could see a very, very sad little Squish sunk into an old wooden chair that looked like it was about to break. There didn't seem to be any one else in the mushroom house, so I decided to knock at the door which looked like it hadn't been painted for at least a hundred years.

I am sad

"Nobody answered so I tried again, this time shouting, "Little Squish, please open the door! I can see that you are sad. Your eyes are leaking onto the floor making big puddles and some of the mice and bugs in there are trying to swim in them. I want to help you."

"The little Squish did not reply, but he did manage to look up at me. His eyes were filled with water and his smile looked like it had been missing for longer than a month. I waited for a while and then asked if he would like some of Grandma Squash's special secret mushroom soup from my mushroom house to help him feel better," Grandpa Squish looked very hopeful.

"Ooooooh, I bet he said yes, Grandpa Squish," said Sausage Pot.

"Well, Sausage Pot, all I could hear were the tiny tears of the little Squish as they fell onto the stone-cold floor," said Grandpa Squish.

"So what did you do?" shouted Winkers very impatiently. Winkers was a lovely little Squish with big beautiful eyelashes. Winkers always wore green with pink spots and he smelt of pineapples.

"Well, Winkers, I decided to go back to Grandma Squash and asked her if she would make me the best bowl of special secret mushroom soup she has ever made," said Grandpa Squish.

"And how did she make the soup even more magical, Grandpa Squish? It has so much magic in it already," said Winkers.

"Well I couldn't tell you exactly how she made the soup. But I can tell you what it looked like?" said Grandpa Squish with a big warm smile.

All of the little Squishes and Squashes slid to the end of their tiny stools and opened their eyes so wide they were almost touching the tops of their fuzzy eyebrows.

Oooooooh how did she make it?

"Well, for starters, the blue floating spots in Grandma Squashes special secret mushroom soup were much bigger than usual, almost the size of the moon. They had an extra special snow-white glow

15

around them, just like the moon when it grins at us. There were so many spots it almost looked like we were having a snow day and the smell of chocolate and ice cream seemed to go up my nose much faster than ever before and it stayed there for a whole week.

"Wow, Grandpa Squish, that is my idea of heaven," said Sausage Pot as he tried to eat the air around him with his eyes closed.

Thank you Grandma Squash

"Once Grandma Squash had made this wonderful concoction I ran down the road as fast as my feet could find the paths," said Grandpa Squish.

"I bet that wasn't very fast was it, Grandpa

Squish?" said Winkers. All of the little Squishes and Squashes squiggled and giggled with laughter.

"Well it was certainly fast for me," said Grandpa Squish, smiling. "I found my way to the sad little Squish's mushroom house again.

With the special soup in my hand, I simply followed the blue floating spots as they led the way.

THREE

Special Secret Mushroom Soup

"**I** got to the house to find the sad little Squish still fixed to the old wooden chair, the mushroom house still smelling of cabbage and cheese," said Grandpa Squish.

"Sounds good to me, Grandpa Squish, I think I would be quite happy there," said Sausage Pot.

"Although the chair looked like it was going to break I think the little Squish felt safe there," said Grandpa Squish.

"How could he feel safe in such an old chair that

was about to break, Grandpa Squish?" said a very small Squish called Tiddlypops.

Squatipops and Tiddlypops

"Well, he had been in this place for such a long time, he had forgotten how it felt when he wasn't sitting there. I think he was scared to move, Tiddlypops. He was scared what might happen if he did," said Grandpa Squish, gently.

Tiddlypops looked concerned. "So what happened next, Grandpa Squish?" he asked.

"Well, Tiddlypops, I started to talk to the little Squish: "Little Squish – I am going to leave some mushroom soup here for you. Please eat it, it has magic in it and the power to bring some sparkle into the dark bits of your home.

Blue floating spots kissing my nose

As I said this, one of the blue floating spots made its way past my face filling my nose with the yummy smell of chocolate and ice cream. It then went up through a tiny gap in the window and travelled toward the little Squish. The smell of chocolate and ice cream soon took away the smell of cheese and cabbage, and the blue floating spot kissed the little squishes tiny nose. I could see that something magical had happened.

Something magical happened

"I waited for a bit to see if the little Squish was going to talk but he didn't move or squeak so I made the decision that I would make my way back home. Before I left, I whispered to the little Squish, "I will come back tomorrow with another bowl for you, a little bigger and even more magical. Goodbye little Squish!" And off I wobbled," said Grandpa Squish.

"So you just left him?" cried Tiddlypops.

I can't believe you left him!

"It is all I could do, Tiddlypops, the sad little Squish had to make the choice for himself whether or not to move from the place he had been sitting for so long. It was something that needed to change inside him and I knew it would take a little time so it was best to leave him be," said Grandpa Squish.

"OOOOOOOOOOOOOH," said all the little Squishes and Squashes with their eyes as big as balloons and tails as high as the sky.

"What needs to change inside him?" asked Windipops. "There are things changing in me all the time – I can feel it in my tummy," all the little Squishes and Squashes were squiggling and giggling with laughter.

"The way that he feels about things and sees things," said Grandpa Squish.

"How does he do that?" shouted Sweet Pea. "Does he have to put on special glasses and a special thinking hat?"

"Let Grandpa Squish tell you," shouted Tiddlypops.

"Thank you, Tiddlypops. Now when the next day came I made my way to the little Squish's mushroom house wondering if there would be an empty bowl and..." said Grandpa Squish.

"And?" said Sausage Pot eating five cherry bake cakes at once.

These are my favourite

"And?" said Windipops trumping with excitement.

"AND?" said the rest of the little Squishes and Squashes in harmony as they slid to the very edge of their tiny stools.

FOUR

What's your name?

*W*ith a deep breath Grandpa Squish announced, "And it was! The bowl was empty!", said Grandpa Squish with huge delight.

All of the little Squishes and Squashes cheered with their biggest squeaks.

"Squippee!" they cried.

"Haha," laughed Grandpa Squish. "Just like you, I was very, very happy and replaced the empty bowl with a slightly bigger brand-new shiny bowl of Grandma Squash's special secret mushroom soup. Then I started to speak: "Little Squish, will you tell me your name? I would love to know it. Shyly and slowly the little Squish looked up," said Grandpa Squish.

My name is….

"My name is Bruni," he said in a very soft voice, "Thank you for the special secret mushroom soup."

"Well hello, Bruni, I thought it was you. They call

me Grandpa Squish and, well, I like to tell stories to all the little Squishes and Squashes of Squishville. Would you like me to tell you one?" said Grandpa Squish.

Bruni shook his heavy head from right to left.

"Maybe another day, then. Do not worry, Bruni, there will be plenty of time for stories later."

So for the next month, I visited the grey mushroom every day with a bowl of Grandma Squash's special secret mushroom soup and in return for the soup all I asked from Bruni was for him to tell me three good things about his day," said Grandpa Squish.

"What do you mean, Grandpa Squish?" said Squatipops, who always sat like a frog. Squatipops was as tall as a giant but unfortunately he was a little bit scared of heights.

"How can it be good if he is stuck in that mushroom house all day with no one to talk to and nothing to do? I think I would be so bored that I would make myself into a hat. My eyes would fill up with water too, poor old Bruni," said Squatipops.

Squatipops

"Well Squatipops," said Grandpa Squish, "Bruni has lots to be thankful for."

Squatipops looked confused.

"Bruni wakes up every morning and when he looks out the window the sun smiles at him. He has the biggest, bushiest tail in the whole of Squishville protecting him and helping him to balance and report any danger that may be close. His mushroom house, although grey, keeps him safe and warm. So if we can help him realise how much he has to be grateful for he will start to see Squishville in a whole new light," said Grandpa Squish.

"AAAAAAAH," said Squatipops and all the little Squishes and Squashes.

Bruni's House

"Everyday I saw something bigger and brighter coming from Bruni. His mushroom began to turn into the brightest of reds like a strawberry-coloured lollipop. It almost started to smell like strawberries topped with a dollop of cream and a dash of chocolate sprinkles.

The sun felt so much good coming from the mushroom house that it sent flying sunbeams straight towards it, making it the biggest most beautiful mushroom you have ever seen," said Grandpa Squish.

That was close

At this point Sweet Pea almost fell off her chair due to excitement.

"Bruni started to look different. He had a wide smile stretched all the way across his fuzzy face and his tail was so fluffy it looked like a big fat cloud of candy floss. Then Bruni started to talk," said Grandpa Squish.

Look for the good stuff

"Dear Grandpa Squish, you have made me see that there is lots of magic in this world. Telling you the

three best things about my day has helped me to look for the positive in everything and you know what Grandpa Squish? There is ALWAYS something positive – you just have to open youreyes and your fuzzy head to see it.

"At first I thought it was silly but I loved Grandma Squash's special secret mushroom so much I thought I would give it a try. Now I see things in a different way, and I don't want to waste any more time sitting in this house. Thank you, Grandpa Squish for giving me the help I needed to see what a magical place Squishville really is," Bruni's eyes were filled with so much joy as he spoke, with happy tears in his eyes.

This soup is magic

"Ah I get it! It was the magic in the mushroom soup that helped Bruni?" said Sweet Pea.

"Yes, Sweet Pea, Grandma's special secret mushroom soup is truly magical," said Grandpa Squish.

"And Grandpa Squish, by Bruni saying three good things about each and every day, he is now able to look for the good rather than the bad things and that helps him be positive and happy, doesn't it?" said Sweet Pea.

"That's exactly it, Sweet Pea," said Grandpa Squish with a big smile.

"I think it's a great story, Grandpa Squish, and well done for helping poor old Bruni," said Sausage Pot, with another bundle of Grandma Squash's cherry bake cakes in his mouth.

"The magic was in Bruni all the time!" cried Squatipops.

Look at the love

"Yes that's it, Squatipops, the magic is within all of us, we just need to learn how to magic it out," said Grandpa Squish as he gave Grandma Squash a great big squishkiss.

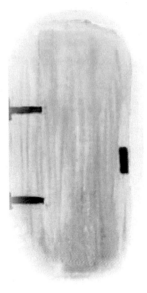

Just then the door opened and there standing in the doorway was… "Bruni!" shouted the little squishes and squashes as they ran toward him and gave him the biggest hug they could find. Sausage Pot then offered him his chair, Bruni gave him the biggest smile and joined the little squirrels around the warm cozy fire as they ate the rest of Grandma Squashes special Cherry bake cakes.

This is NEARLY the end….

Binky Bonk and Stinky Stonk

Meet these characters in the next book…..

Please turn over for The Most Top Secret Squirrel Mission….

The Most Top Secret Squirrel Mission

SHHHHHH!

You must tell absolutely NO ONE about this secret mission!

It is MOST TOP SECRET!

Once completed you can tell your family and friends and help them through the mission.

Turn over for all SECRET squirrel instructions.

Do this quietly (SHHHHH) It needs to be a secret even from your pets!

The Mission

- Your mission is to write down 3 things you have enjoyed about your day. You can write more than 3 but definitely not less.
- Do this for 21 whole days !

What will happen if I do this?

Magical things happen in the brain that help you to look for the positive in each and every day, just like it helped Bruni.

GOOD LUCK!

My Thank you's

I would like to say a huge big thank you to Ann Foo for all of her wonderful illustrations in the book. Thank you to Charlotte Ketteridge for your gorgeous book cover design & help throughout.

A big round of applause to my gorgeous niece Lilly Foo Black for helping me find some of my favourite squirrels. To Lisa Edwards for your excellent copy editing skills.

A HUGE squishy squashy thank you to Clive Ketteridge for believing in Squishville.

Not to forget the HUGE support of my wonderful family and friends.

Great BIG LOVE to you all.......

About the Author

I found Squishville while walking in the woods at the end of my garden one morning, I was so inspired by this enchanted little village that I wanted to share it with you.

I believe that there are lots of secret magic places hidden in the world that have yet to be discovered, you might even have one in your garden! The secret in finding one is to always be on the look out for magic, as it may lie in the places you least expect.

Taira Foo is an emerging author of childrens books. This is the first book in the series of 'The Magical Adventures of Squishville.'

Always look for the magic, as it may be right beside you
....

Made in the USA
Middletown, DE
28 October 2021